TO ME WAY-AY-AY-YAH!

We'll all throw dirt at the cook!

from the short-drag chantey "Paddy Doyle"

NEW CASTLE COUNTY

Come, all ye young sailormen, listen to me,

I'll sing you a song of the fish of the sea.

Then blow ye winds westerly, westerly blow,

from the fo'c'sle ballad "The Boston Come-All-Ye"

WE'RE BOUND TO THE SOUTH-'ARD,

SO STEADY SHE GOES!

LOUD EMILY

ALEXIS O'NEILL

PICTURES BY

NANCY CARPENTER

SIMON & SCHUSTER BOOKS FOR YOUNG READERS

For David, my WZRDJG, with all my love
(and with thanks to all the Emilys)

—A.O.

In honor of all the unknown artists of the nineteenth century,
and for Gia, certain to be a well-known artist
of the next century

—N.C.

SIMON & SCHUSTER BOOKS FOR YOUNG READERS
An imprint of Simon & Schuster Children's Publishing Division
1230 Avenue of the Americas, New York, New York 10020

Text copyright © 1998 by Alexis O'Neill
Illustrations copyright © 1998 by Nancy Carpenter
All rights reserved including the right of reproduction in whole or in part in any form.
SIMON & SCHUSTER BOOKS FOR YOUNG READERS is a trademark of Simon & Schuster.
Book design by Heather Wood. The text of this book is set in Cheltenham.
The illustrations are rendered in oil paint.
Printed in Hong Kong
First Edition
3 5 7 9 10 8 6 4 2

Library of Congress Cataloging-in-Publication Data
O'Neill, Alexis, 1949–
Loud Emily / written by Alexis O'Neill ; illustrated by Nancy Carpenter.
p.   cm.
Summary : A little girl with a big voice who lives in a nineteenth-century whaling town
finds a way to be useful and happy aboard a sailing ship.
ISBN 0-689-81078-4
[1. Voice—Fiction. 2. Sea stories.] I. Carpenter, Nancy, ill. II. Title
PZ7.O5523Lo   1998   [E]—dc21   97-18217

The songs on the endpapers and others like them can be found in *Songs of the American Sailormen*
by Joanna C. Colcord (W.W. Norton & Co., Inc., 1938) and *The Music of the Waters* by Laura Alexandrine Smith
(Kegan Paul, Trench & Co., 1888).

SAILORS' TERMS AND PHRASES

Ahoy!
Attention!

All hands on deck!
Everyone must come up to the top platform of the ship!

Avast!
Stop what you're doing!

Aye, aye!
Yes!

bosun (boatswain)
whistle-carrying officer in charge of deck crew

bowsprit
pole extending forward from the ship

cooper
person who makes wooden barrels

chantey
song sung by sailors to the rhythm of their movements while working
Different kinds of chanteys—short-drag, capstan, and halyard—were sung for different kinds of work.

fo'c'sle (forecastle)
section of the upper deck located at the front of the ship
A fo'c'sle ballad is a story sung when the crew was off-duty.

Furl the main and stop it down!
Roll up the main sail and tie it down with short lines of rope!

halyard
rope for hoisting or lowering a sail or a flag
"Blow the Man Down" is a famous halyard chantey.

Luff her up before we're stove!
Steer our ship into the wind so the sails flap, or else we'll crash!

mizzenmast
third mast back on a sailing ship

quarter-deck
back part of a sailing ship, usually reserved for officers

rigger
person who fits a system of ropes, chains, and tackles used to support masts, sails, and yards of a sailing vessel

smithy
person who works in a blacksmith shop, making items out of iron with an anvil and a hammer

swabbing
mopping

tiller
lever used to turn a rudder and steer a ship

From the moment of birth Emily's voice boomed.

"GOO GOO BA BA!" Emily sang in her Emily voice.

It startled the midwife. It astonished the neighbors. It frightened the birds that were nesting in trees.

Emily's parents loved her truly, but oh, dear! Her voice could be heard 'round that seaside town!

"Perhaps she'll grow out of it," said her father as he closed all the windows and fastened the doors.

"We can only hope," said her mother as she covered her ears with embroidered pillows.

But as Emily grew, so did her voice. It rattled the brasses. It shimmied the crystals. It shattered the plates as they crashed to the floor.

"GOOD MORNING!" Emily said in her Emily voice.

"Please be soft," said Father.

"GOOD AFTERNOON!" Emily said in her Emily voice.

"Please do whisper," said Mother.

"I'M READY FOR LESSONS!" Emily said in her Emily voice.

"You *must* be *quiet*," snapped the tutor, who threatened to quit.

When Emily turned seven, she heard Father fretting, "How will she find her way in the world?"

Mother sighed, "How will she find friends?"

The tutor hissed, "How can I teach such a boisterous child?"

"I'LL TRY HARDER," Emily vowed in her Emily voice. Emily slipped back into the hallway. Her lonely footsteps echoed on the polished floor. She wandered past the grand staircase and tiptoed down by the in-and-out door. Emily tweaked it open a crack. Oh! She heard pots and pans banging, cupboard doors slamming, errand boys yelling, "Deliveries ho!"

Emily stepped inside and tugged at the skirts of the kitchen's round cook.

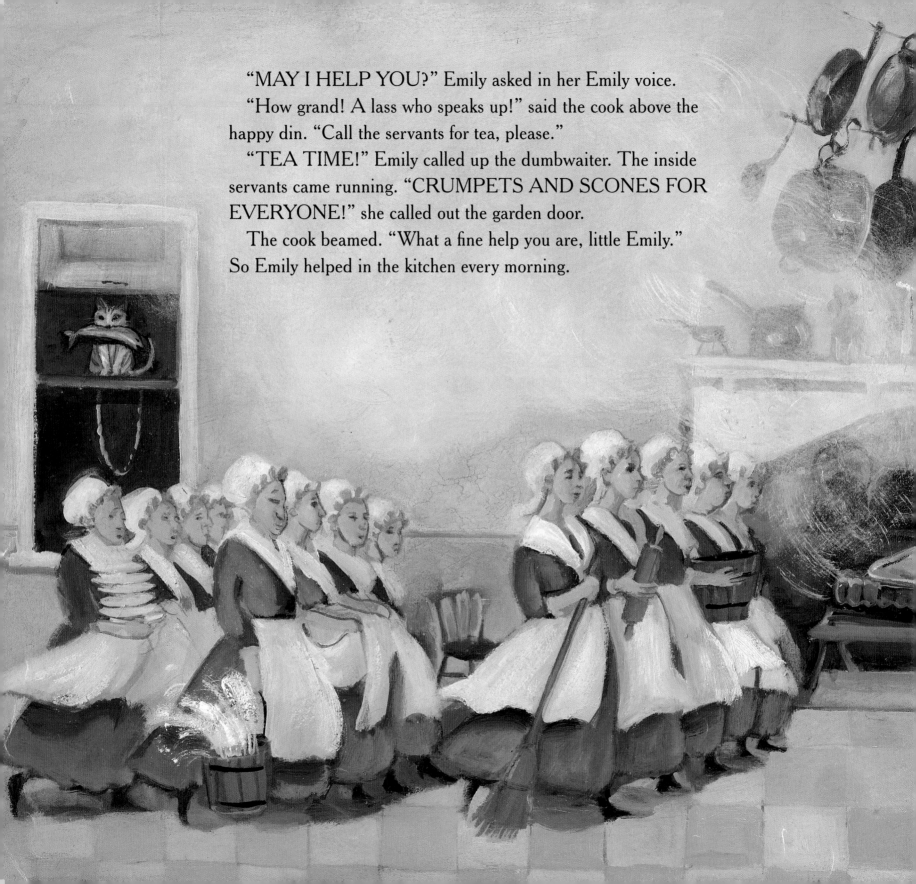

"MAY I HELP YOU?" Emily asked in her Emily voice.

"How grand! A lass who speaks up!" said the cook above the happy din. "Call the servants for tea, please."

"TEA TIME!" Emily called up the dumbwaiter. The inside servants came running. "CRUMPETS AND SCONES FOR EVERYONE!" she called out the garden door.

The cook beamed. "What a fine help you are, little Emily." So Emily helped in the kitchen every morning.

Upstairs, her parents still worried.

"What about a boarding school?" her father wondered.

"A boarding school?" her mother asked.

"Yes, she must go to a boarding school," crowed the tutor, "far across the sea! And may I suggest Miss Meekmeister's School for Soft-Spoken Girls?"

Emily tried to be happy. But a misty grayness crept inside her and would not go away.

On the day before Emily was to set sail, the cook took her hand. "Come, little Emily. Before you go, come with me to Front Street and help me buy some nice fresh fish."

Emily heard Front Street before she saw it. Oh! What a lovely place it was, there among the tall ships. The salty air rang with the sounds of riggers and smithies and coopers at work. Sailors trundled cargo along wooden wharves. Carriages thundered up cobblestone streets. Crowds burst from taverns with songs on their lips.

"I LOVE IT HERE!" Emily said in her Emily voice. As Emily skipped along the wharf, she saw a small notice tacked to a large ship.

LOUD HELP NEEDED.
NOW.
CASTING OFF TODAY.
Captain Baroo

"Ahoy there," called the first mate to Emily. "Are you loud?"

"I AM!" answered Emily.

"Come aboard, then," he said.

And Emily did.

She walked up the rickety plank and right into Captain Baroo.

"MY NAME IS EMILY," Emily said in her Emily voice. "HOW CAN I HELP?"

"Can you call an order from the fo'c'sle to quarter-deck above a gale force wind?" peeped Captain Baroo.

"AYE AYE, CAPTAIN!" she said.

Before the captain could say "Mizzenmast," Emily called, "ALL HANDS ON DECK!" and every ship's crew came running.

"Welcome aboard, Emily," cheeped Captain Baroo.

Emily waved to the cook as the ship left the harbor. "TELL MY PARENTS I'M ALL BOARDED," she called. "TELL THEM I WILL WRITE." Her voice made waves in the sea.

Captain Baroo's crew was kind and luckless. But how they loved
Emily's voice! She sang halyard chanteys while hoisting the sails.
She called bosun's commands while standing the watch. She told
stories to the crew while swabbing the deck. From her tidy bunk
at night she crooned fo'c'sle ballads that made the men cry.

And deep out in the ocean the whales listened, too. They danced
to her wild tunes. They sang with her free songs. They spouted and
blew their delight in the air.

One day, a storm lifted waves into walls of water and shivered the
timbers of the very old ship. Captain Baroo whispered commands
into Emily's ear.

Emily shouted, "AVAST! LUFF HER UP BEFORE WE'RE
STOVE!"

The men scrambled into the riggings as the ship pitched and
plunged and dove into the raging sea.

She cried, "FURL THE MAIN AND STOP IT DOWN!"

The wind screamed its fury as Captain Baroo and his raggedy
crew rolled up the sails. All day and all night they fought the wild
and thundering waves. They kept the ship safe until the storm finally
moved on. "At last." The captain sighed.

But when morning came, fog rolled in like a blanket of blubber.
"Can't see a thing!" complained Captain Baroo.
"Neither can we!" moaned his poor tired crew, and they fell fast
asleep on the deck.
Emily peered over the railing.

Rocks! The ship was racing fast toward a rough, jagged shore. Where was the lighthouse? Had the fierce storm destroyed it?

"AHOY!" Emily called in her Emily voice. "AHOY! AHOY!" But nothing could wake the snoring crew. She pulled at the tiller but the ship wouldn't turn. What could she do?

And then she remembered the whales.

Emily rushed to the bowsprit and shimmied along. Into the waves she cast her voice until a ribbon of bubbles carried her words into the briny deep: "DANGER! PLEASE HELP! DANGER! PLEASE HELP!" She sang in song for the whales. And as Emily sang, the whales gathered 'round. They hastened from Baja, they raced down from Iceland, they speeded their way from the tip of Cape Horn. Then, as if the ship were one of their own, they nuzzled her and cradled her and eased her away from the treacherous coast.

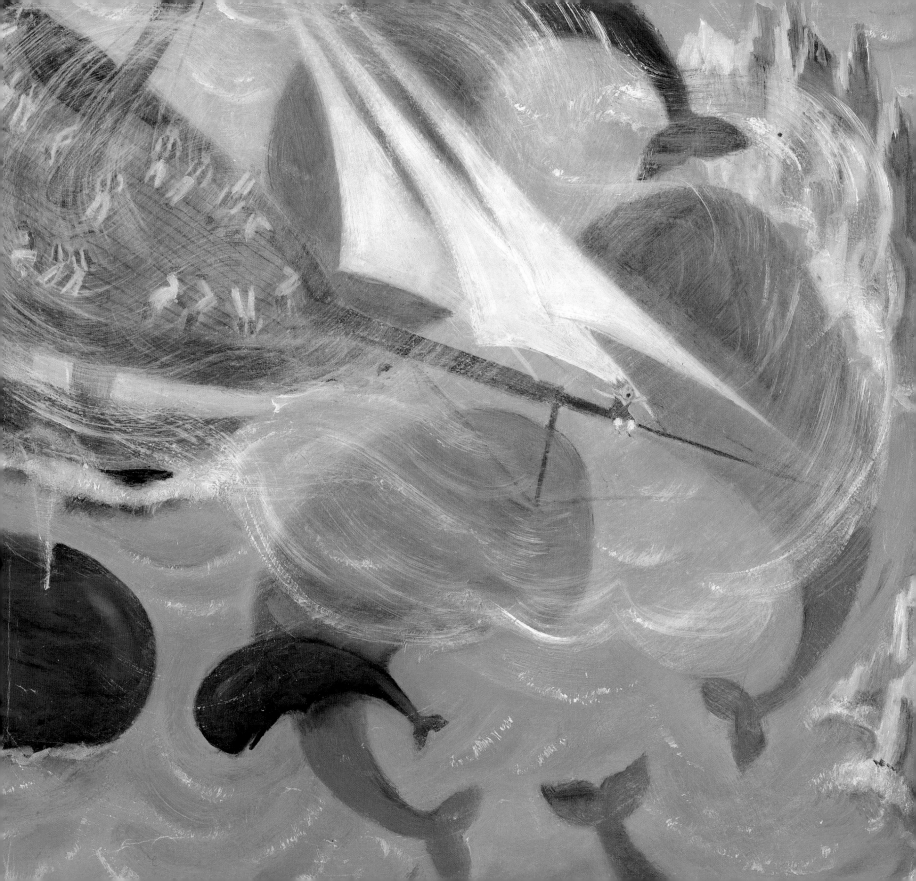

Emily sighed. Safe! But the other ships from the seaside town . . . they faced danger, too. So she called once again to her friends of the sea. Between rolling waves and hazardous rocks the whales formed a long bridge, the whales formed a wide bridge, and Emily ran from her ship to the shore. Up the winding lighthouse stairs she scrambled and took her deepest, deepest breath.

"DaaaaaaaanGER! ROCKS heeeeeere!" she called.

"Rocks HEEEEEEEERE! DAAAAANger!"

Over and over she sang her two-note warning:

"DaaaaaaaanGER! ROCKS heeeeeere!"

"Rocks HEEEEEEEERE! DAAAAANger!"

Emily's voice rang out loud and true. Her call pierced the thick fog, her voice tamed the fierce waves, and the captains and crews turned their ships back to sea.

Soon the sun shone in the wide sky. On the horizon were ships and ships and ships, far from the threatening rocks. Along the shore stood all the folks of the city shouting HURRAH! for the little girl with the very big voice. The happiest shouts of all came from her own proud parents.

Now Emily lives with her parents and the kitchen's round cook in a home near the lighthouse on top of the rocks. On sunny days Emily does what little girls do. But on foggy days, and on stormy days, and on very windy days, Emily cautions all ships in her loudest Emily voice and keeps them safe from harm.

And nobody there in that house by the sea ever complains of the noise.

AUTHOR'S NOTE

Loud Emily's stately home would have been above a busy harbor—quite possibly in New Bedford, Massachusetts, during the 1850s. On her walk with the cook, Emily would have seen mostly whaling ships because at that time New England was the whaling capital of the world. In fact, during peak years, more than 700 whalers sailed from the New England coast. These ships were over 100 feet long and carried a crew of up to thirty-five men. A typical voyage might have lasted from two to five years and might have taken the crew to the warm South Seas or to frigid Arctic waters. The places from which the whalers departed—Nantucket, New London, Sag Harbor, Stonington, and others—grew in size and wealth as a result of the whaling industry.

People of the nineteenth century depended on whale products for many everyday uses. Whale bone was made into items such as fishing poles, buttons, umbrella ribs, and skirt hoops. Whale oil was used for lubricating machinery and lighting lamps in homes and lighthouses. Spermaceti, a fatty substance, was used in making smokeless candles. Ambergris, a waxy gray material, was used in perfumes. As soon as substitutes were discovered, such as petroleum in Pennsylvania in 1859, whaling in America began to decline, and the industry finally disappeared after World War I.

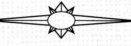

ILLUSTRATOR'S NOTE

The paintings for *Loud Emily* were inspired by the works of American folk artists who flourished in the first half of the nineteenth century. These self-taught artists would sometimes travel from town to town offering to paint portraits and scenes for a fee. A simpler picture, say one that was flat with little shadow, would cost less. More elaborate paintings might be as much as ten dollars apiece. In prosperous places such as the New England whaling towns, people were spending more to decorate their homes with such paintings. The sailors who docked in these towns were often artists in their own right, as they spent the long hours at sea carving pictures onto whalebone, an art form known as scrimshaw. The endpapers for *Loud Emily* are done in the style of scrimshaw carvings.

Around the same time that whaling began to decline in America, so too did the popularity of portrait painting. Folk painters fell on hard times as a new technology—photography—became widespread. Many portrait painters had to find other work as people became eager to have more realistic pictures of themselves, which were also less expensive than a painting.

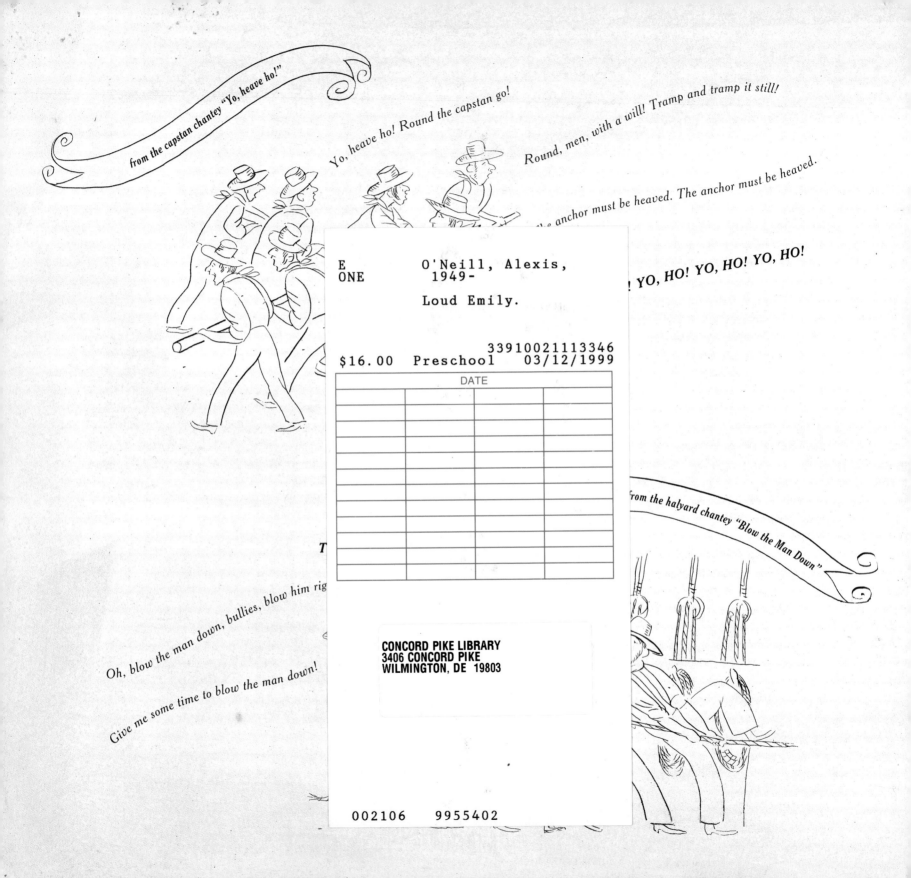

from the capstan chantey "Yo, heave ho!"

Yo, heave ho! Round the capstan go!

Round, men, with a will! Tramp and tramp it still!

The anchor must be heaved. The anchor must be heaved.

YO, HO! YO, HO! YO, HO!

from the halyard chantey "Blow the Man Down"

Oh, blow the man down, bullies, blow him right down!

Give me some time to blow the man down!